P9-DDY-723

WELCOME TO
PASSPORT TO READING
A beginning reader's ticket to a brand-new world!

Every book in this program is designed to build read-along and read-alone skills, level by level, through engaging and enriching stories. As the reader turns each page, he or she will become more confident with new vocabulary, sight words, and comprehension.

These PASSPORT TO READING levels will help you choose the perfect book for every reader.

READING TOGETHER
Read short words in simple sentence structures together to begin a reader's journey.

READING OUT LOUD
Encourage developing readers to sound out words in more complex stories with simple vocabulary.

READING INDEPENDENTLY
Newly independent readers gain confidence reading more complex sentences with higher word counts.

READY TO READ MORE
Readers prepare for chapter books with fewer illustrations and longer paragraphs.

This book features sight words from the educator-supported Dolch Sight Words List. This encourages the reader to recognize commonly used vocabulary words, increasing reading speed and fluency.

For more information, please visit passporttoreadingbooks.com.

Enjoy the journey!

Little, Brown and Company

Hachette Book Group
1290 Avenue of the Americas, New York, NY 10104
Visit us at lb-kids.com

Little, Brown and Company is a division of Hachette Book Group, Inc.
The Little, Brown name and logo are trademarks of Hachette Book Group, Inc.
The publisher is not responsible for websites (or their content) that are not owned by the publisher.

First Edition: August 2016

Library of Congress Cataloging-in-Publication Data
Names: King, Trey, author.
Title: Training Academy : construction! / by Trey King.
Other titles: At head of title: Transformers rescue bots
Description: First edition. | New York ; Boston : Little, Brown Books for Young Readers, 2016. | Series: Passport to reading. Level 2
Identifiers: LCCN 2015036110| ISBN 9780316389730 (paperback) | ISBN 9780316389747 (ebook) | ISBN 9780316389754 (library edition ebook)
Subjects: | BISAC: JUVENILE FICTION / Action & Adventure / General. | JUVENILE FICTION / Media Tie-In. | JUVENILE FICTION / Science Fiction. | JUVENILE FICTION / Toys, Dolls, Puppets.
Classification: LCC PZ7.K589175 Trc 2016 | DDC [E]—dc23
LC record available at http://lccn.loc.gov/2015036110

10 9 8 7 6 5 4 3 2 1
CW

Printed in the United States of America

Passport to Reading titles are leveled by independent reviewers applying the standards developed by Irene Fountas and Gay Su in *Matching Books to Readers: Using Leveled Books in Guided Reading*, Heinemann, 1999.

Licensed By:

Page 3 photo of construction workers © Kurhan/Shutterstock.com; page 6 photo of home © Katarzyna Wojtasik/Shutterstock.c page 6 photo of library ©ValeStock/Getty Images; page 6 photo of road © Dolly MJ/Shutterstock.com; page 6 photo of schoo Cynthia Farmer/Shutterstock.com; page 7 photo of office buildings © Ant Clausen/Shutterstock.com; page 7 photo of museum Osugi/Shutterstock.com; page 7 photo of sidewalk © Alison Hancock/Shutterstock.com; page 7 photo of bridge © Anton Fo Shutterstock.com; page 8 photo of bulldozer © gregg Cerenzio/Shutterstock.com; page 9, 32 photo of bulldozer track © TSpi Shutterstock.com; page 10 photo of dump truck © TFoxFoto/Shutterstock.com; page 11 photo of dump truck with excavator Paul Vasarhelyi/Shutterstock.com; page 12 top photo of loader © Four Oaks/Shutterstock.com; page 12 bottom photo of loa © mihalec/Shutterstock.com; page 13 photo of backhoe © Dmitry Kalinovsky/Shutterstock.com; page 13 photo of ripper © Ar Photo UK/Shutterstock.com; page 14 photo of crane © mihalec/Shutterstock.com; page 15, 32 photo of wrecking ball and demolis building © EdgeOfReason/Shutterstock.com; page 16 photo of cement truck © Richard Thornton/Shutterstock.com; page 16 ph of man pouring cement © Christina Richards/Shutterstock.com; page 17 photo of road roller © Vadim Ratnikov/Shutterstock.c page 18 photo of crane © vvoe/Shutterstock.com; page 18 photo of excavator © ownway/Shutterstock.com; page 18 photo of du truck © Gualberto Becerra/Shutterstock.com; page 19 photo of cement truck © 6493866629 /Shutterstock.com; page 19 phot bulldozer © ronin3ds/Shutterstock.com; page 19 photo of loader © Karen Katrjyan/Shutterstock.com; page 19 photo of road rolle David Touchtone/Shutterstock.com; page 20 photo of tunnel © Luca Flor/Shutterstock.com; page 20 photo of bridge © MarchCat Shutterstock.com; page 20 photo of dam © Andrew Zarivny/Shutterstock.com; page 21, 32 photo of park © John A. Anders Shutterstock.com; page 21 photo of giraffe © Thitisan/Shutterstock.com; page 22 photo of pyramid © posztos/Shutterst com; page 22 photo of Colosseum © Iakov Kalinin/Shutterstock.com; page 23 photo of crane with skyline © Serhii Bol Shutterstock.com; page 23 photo of man on the left © LifetimeStock/Shutterstock.com; page 23 photo of man in the middle © Phov Shutterstock.com; page 23 photo of woman on the right © studioloco/Shutterstock.com; page 24, 32 photo of architects © Poznyak Shutterstock.com; page 25 photo of construction workers © Andreas G. Karelias/Shutterstock.com; page 25 photo of plumber Dmitry Kalinovsky/Shutterstock.com; page 25 photo of electrician © Phovoir/Shutterstock.com; pages 26—27 photo of snow plow Pi-Lens/Shutterstock.com; page 28 photo of bulldozer © Four Oaks/Shutterstock.com; page 28—29 photo of forest fire © Arnold J Labrentz/Shutterstock.com; page 30 photo of London © TTstudio/Shutterstock.com; page 30 photo of Washington, DC © S.Boris Shutterstock.com; page 30 photo of Seoul © Sean Pavone/Shutterstock.com

TRAINING ACADEMY

CONSTRUCTION!

by Trey King

LITTLE, BROWN AND COMPANY
New York   Boston

"I am making another manual for the Rescue Bots Training Academy," Cody says "This time it is about **construction**."

"That is a big topic," Graham says.

"There are so many construction vehicles.

Each one does something different, too.

Some are used for tearing things down.

Others build new things,

and some help people."

"And some do all three!"

Boulder says.

"All the buildings and structures you see are built by construction workers and their vehicles," Graham says. Here are just a few examples:

Homes

Roads and highways

Libraries

Schools

Office buildings

Sidewalks

Museums

Bridges

That IS a lot! Where should we start?

Let us start by talking about a vehicle you know very well, Cody.... A bulldozer—like me!

7

Bulldozers are mighty vehicles made to move or demolish everything in their path. They can move dirt and trash or help knock down buildings. These powerful machines are used by builders, farmers, and even soldiers!

Many bulldozers have tracks instead of wheels, just like tanks.

This makes bulldozers move slower, but tracks also make them much stronger.

9

Another powerful construction vehicle
is a **dump truck**.
On its back is a boxy container called a bed.
But there is no sleeping here—not unless
you want to be dumped out with a bunch
of dirt!

Dump trucks are perfect for moving heavy things—like building supplies, such as gravel, sand, dirt, and lumber. They are also great for hauling scrap and trash away.

One of the best ways to load a dump truck is with an **excavator**!
These large diggers use steel ropes and arms to dig holes, create trenches, and help with mining.

"Is that another bulldozer? Cody asks.

"Actually, that is a loader," Boulder explains
Bulldozers are good at pushing and shoving.
Loaders are better at
scooping and lifting.
They can load rocks,
sand, trash, and other
materials into dump
trucks or onto
conveyor belts.

Heavy equipment vehicles also can have more than one use.

Some loaders have a backhoe, a small bucket on the back end.

Others have a ripper, which is used to tear up the ground or street.

Backhoe

Ripper

The tallest of all construction vehicles is the **crane**.

Using a system of ropes, wires, and chains, it is able to lift or lower heavy objects and move them from one place to another.

FUN FACT

The first known construction cranes were used by the ancient Greeks! They were often powered by men and donkeys!

Demolition means taking
something apart.
One of the most useful demolition
tools is a **wrecking ball**.

A wrecking ball is a heavy steel ball
that is usually hung from a crane.
It is often used to break down big buildings
that are no longer in use.

A **cement truck** has a large drum on its back that spins around and around, slowly mixing cement, sand or gravel, and water to make wet concrete. When it is ready, construction workers pour it out to make sidewalks and roads.

16

Then a **road roller** rolls over the wet concrete to make sure the surface is smooth and flat.
This action creates safe roads.

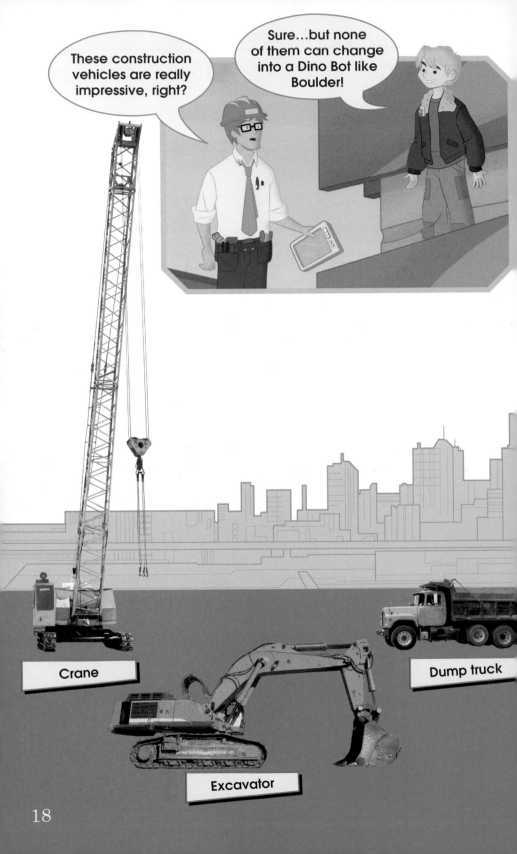

There are dozens of different kinds of
vehicles used for construction.
Some lay pipes while others drill holes.
Each one has a specific use.
But one thing is true about all of them—
they are used to help people build!

Bulldozer

Road roller

Cement truck

Loader

Construction vehicles and workers build almost everything you see.

They build houses and businesses.

They build bridges, tunnels, and dams, too.

Tunnel

Dam

Bridge

They even help build zoos and city parks.

It feels good to create a living space for all creatures on the planet.

People have been constructing—or building—things for a very long time. The pyramids in Egypt were built almost 5,000 years ago!

You can think of the ancient Colosseum in Rome as one of the first football stadiums. It was built to hold almost 90,000 people so they could watch live sports, games, and races!

These days, we have all kinds of tools and vehicles to help us construct amazing buildings, like skyscrapers.

There is a whole team of people who work on just one building. **Architects** design the buildings. They make blueprints, which are drawings that instruct others on how to build.

Architects are a lot like engineers because they design AND build structures.

Construction workers build the buildings.

Plumbers add piping so that buildings can have bathrooms and kitchens.

Electricians install the wires and electricity so the building has power.

Construction vehicles do more than just build things—they also help in emergencies!

When it snows a lot, people can
become trapped.
If a snowplow is attached to the
front of a tractor or dump truck,
it can clear the snow out of the way!

Bulldozers are often used to stop forest fires.

They dig trenches and knock down trees to stop fires from spreading.

29

"Wow, I sure learned a lot today," Cody says.
"Every major city, and even Griffin Rock,
was built by construction!"

"Pretty much," Graham says.

"That is why our jobs are so important."

London

Washington, DC

Seoul

"I am happy to have a teammate like you, Graham," adds Boulder.

"I hope this book will help new Rescue Bots understand our world," Cody says. "I wonder what my next training subject should be about."

I have an idea!

Hello, Rescue Team cadets!
Go back and read this story again—
but this time, see if you can find these words

Tracks

Wrecking ball

City parks

Architects